W0037774

TO:

FROM:

Copyright © 2019 by Sourcebooks
Text by Erin Guendelsberger
Illustrations by Mattia Cerato

Internal images © Getty Images/juliahenderson, Getty Images/AndreaAstes,
Shutterstock/IM_photo, Shutterstock/Luciano Mortula - LGM, Shutterstock/
Christopher Manzeck, Shutterstock/Irene Wang, Shutterstock/VIIIPhotography,
Shutterstock/Michael Gordon, Shutterstock/TTstudio, Shutterstock/Leonard
Zhukovsky

Published by Sourcebooks Wonderland, an imprint of Sourcebooks Kids.
P.O. Box 4410, Naperville, Illinois 60567-4410
(630) 961-3900
sourcebookskids.com

Library of Congress Cataloging-in-Publication Data is on file with the publisher.

Source of Production: 1010 Printing Asia Limited, North Point, Hong Kong, China
Date of Production: May 2019
Run Number: 5014962

Printed and bound in China.
OGP 10 9 8 7 6 5 4 3 2 1

HIDE AND SEEK
NEW YORK

BY ERIN GUENDELSBERGER   PICTURES BY MATTIA CERATO

THE NEW YORK PUBLIC LIBRARY — 4

6 — CHELSEA MARKET

THE AMERICAN MUSEUM OF NATURAL HISTORY — 8

10 — GRAND CENTRAL TERMINAL

CENTRAL PARK — 12

14 — THE NEW YORK AQUARIUM

TIMES SQUARE — 16

18 — BRIGHTON BEACH

JOHN F. KENNEDY INTERNATIONAL AIRPORT — 20

22 — THE BRONX ZOO

sourcebooks wonderland

WELCOME TO NEW YORK CITY—THE BEST CITY IN THE WORLD!

I'm the mayor of this beautiful city, and I need your help. I'm creating an exhibit to feature the greatest parts of New York City, and I am sending YOU on a quest to find the items that represent these places! This chart has everything you need to keep an eye out for and where you need to look.

PREPARE TO BE AMAZED—YOU'RE ABOUT TO EXPLORE AND LEARN ABOUT SOME OF THE BEST MUSEUMS, PARKS, AND ATTRACTIONS THE WORLD HAS EVER SEEN!

MAYOR

THE NEW YORK
PUBLIC LIBRARY

CHELSEA MARKET

JOHN F. KENNEDY
INTERNATIONAL AIRPORT

TIMES SQUARE

BRIGHTON BEACH

CENTRAL PARK

$8.99

THE NEW YORK AQUARIUM

GRAND CENTRAL
TERMINAL

THE BRONX ZOO

THE AMERICAN MUSEUM
OF NATURAL HISTORY

THE NEW YORK PUBLIC LIBRARY

Founded in 1895, the **NEW YORK PUBLIC LIBRARY** is the largest public library system in the U.S. Former governor Samuel J. Tilden donated **$2.4 MILLION** in 1886 to create a free library for the city. After $9 million and sixteen years to design and complete, the library opened on May 24, 1911, to nearly **50,000** visitors.

Today, the **NEW YORK PUBLIC LIBRARY** includes eighty-eight neighborhood branches throughout Manhattan, the Bronx, and Staten Island, plus four scholarly research centers. The library's historical collection includes Christopher Columbus's **1493 LETTER** announcing his discovery of the New World, George Washington's original farewell address, and a copy of the **DECLARATION OF INDEPENDENCE** handwritten by Thomas Jefferson.

CAN YOU FIND...

NOW THAT YOU'RE HERE, COULD YOU HELP ME FIND A FEW OTHER ITEMS?

CHELSEA MARKET

CHELSEA MARKET is an indoor food and shopping market that attracts six million visitors per year. This square block near the **HUDSON RIVER** was originally used by the **ALGONQUIN PEOPLES** for trading game and crops. In 1890, eight large bakeries established the **NEW YORK BISCUIT COMPANY** at the site. In 1898, the company joined with over **100 BAKERIES**, forming the **NATIONAL BISCUIT COMPANY**. After the company moved production to New Jersey in 1958, the Chelsea site fell into disuse. In the 1990s, investor **IRWIN B. COHEN** organized a group to buy the land and transform it into what is now **CHELSEA MARKET**.

Visitors to Chelsea Market, found between 9th and 10th Avenues and 15th and 16th Streets, can enjoy more than **35 VENDORS** selling goods like soup, coffee, cheesecake, nuts, baked goods, cheese, and more.

CAN YOU FIND...

THE AMERICAN MUSEUM OF NATURAL HISTORY

The **AMERICAN MUSEUM OF NATURAL HISTORY** was founded on April 6, 1869, and a series of exhibits opened at **CENTRAL PARK ARSENAL** in 1871. After outgrowing the space, the museum moved to a new building and opened to the public in 1877. From the late 1800s through the 1930s, museum representatives participated in expeditions to every continent and discovered the **NORTH POLE**.

Visitors today can see exhibits about plants, animals, space, human origins, dinosaurs, gems, minerals, and more. An exhibit hall featuring ocean life includes one of the museum's most famous displays—a 21,000 pound blue whale hung from the ceiling. The museum also has the world's highest freestanding dinosaur display—a five-story-high **BAROSAURUS** cast! Kids can also participate in special **"NIGHT AT THE MUSEUM"** sleepovers in the fossil halls.

CAN YOU FIND...

WOW, THERE'S A LOT HERE! CAN YOU HELP ME FIND THESE THINGS?

GRAND CENTRAL TERMINAL

GRAND CENTRAL TERMINAL opened in 1913 to replace a station constructed by three railroad companies. Entrepreneur **CORNELIUS VANDERBILT** bought and consolidated these companies, and Grand Central was built to handle the increasing railroad traffic. But as railroad travel eventually declined with the rise of cars and airplanes, the terminal fell into disrepair. It was almost torn down several times but was restored in the 1990s.

Today, **GRAND CENTRAL TERMINAL** is a landmark site for shopping, dining, and cultural events, as well as railway and subway travel, visited by about **750,000 PEOPLE** every day. The terminal features a grand, cathedral-like ceiling, the famous information booth clock, and a **WHISPERING GALLERY**, "an acoustical phenomenon" that lets two people on opposite sides of the room hear each other.

CAN YOU FIND...

CENTRAL PARK

World-famous **CENTRAL PARK** is a New York City icon that spans an impressive **843 ACRES**. During the early 1800s, when New York's population was booming and city planners rushed to lay the blueprints for modern New York, those plans only allowed for small park areas. That all changed when, in 1853, state officials approved funds for the purchase of land between 5th and 8th Avenues. Construction began in 1858, and over the next fifteen years, workers built **36 ARCHES AND BRIDGES**, moved five million cubic tons of earth, planted half a billion trees and shrubs, and hand-crafted each of Central Park's landscapes. After almost two decades, the park opened to massive public approval. Now, Central Park is the most frequently visited city park in the U.S. with more than **42 MILLION VISITORS** each year!

CAN YOU FIND...

THE NEW YORK AQUARIUM

THE NEW YORK AQUARIUM is the oldest continually operating aquarium in the United States. It first opened on December 10, 1896, in Battery Park's Castle Clinton in Lower Manhattan. The aquarium relocated to **CONEY ISLAND** in 1941 and opened on the Coney Island boardwalk on June 6, 1957. In 1992, a 10 x 332 ft. concrete sculpture called **"SYMPHONY OF THE SEA"** was installed on the boardwalk outside the aquarium.

Visitors to the aquarium today can see penguin and sea otter feedings as well as a sea lion show. The aquarium is home to more than **350 SPECIES** of aquatic wildlife and **8,000 INDIVIDUAL SEA CREATURES**, including cownose rays, green moray eels, California sea lions, sea otters, black-footed penguins, harbor seals, pacific walruses, turtles, and sand tiger sharks.

CAN YOU FIND...

$8.99

TIMES SQUARE

In the late 1880s, **LONG ACRE SQUARE** was the site for William H. Vanderbilt's American Horse Exchange—a large open area surrounded by apartments. The square began to grow and change when **ELECTRICITY** was introduced and New York's first rapid transit system was built. Suddenly, there were streetlights, advertisements, and a lot of people! When the *New York Times* built **TIMES TOWER** on the square, it was the second tallest building in New York, and the square's name was officially changed from Long Acre to **TIMES SQUARE**. In 1905, the newspaper staged a celebration on **NEW YEAR'S EVE** to commemorate the new building. This tradition continues today, with large crowds gathering at Times Square every **DECEMBER 31ST**. Times Square continues to be a hub for entertainment, with hundreds of theaters, restaurants, stores, hotels, museums, and attractions.

CAN YOU FIND...

MUSICAL

WHILE YOU'RE HERE, CAN YOU ALSO FIND THESE OBJECTS?

BRIGHTON BEACH

BRIGHTON BEACH, named after a famous English beach town, was created by entrepreneur **WILLIAM A. ENGEMAN**. He built a small wooden pier in 1869, opened a hotel in 1871, and built the two-story **BRIGHTON BEACH BATHING PAVILION** and **OCEAN PIER** in 1878. Early in Brighton Beach's history, the sea started to rise, threatening the **BRIGHTON BEACH HOTEL** and other businesses. In 1888, engineers placed 125 iron flat cars under the 6,000-ton hotel and used six train engines and 24 iron rails to move it 600 feet inland. In 1905, a mile-long boardwalk opened at **BRIGHTON BEACH PARK**—including a wild animal arena, scenic railway, carousel, fairground, and pavilion.

Visitors to the beach today can enjoy the iconic boardwalk, sand, water, and an assortment of Eastern European shops and restaurants. There is surfing, biking, and skating as well.

CAN YOU FIND...

JOHN F. KENNEDY INTERNATIONAL AIRPORT

Construction for a new international airport for **NEW YORK CITY** began in 1942 at the site of the **IDLEWILD GOLF COURSE** in Queens. The airport opened on June 1, 1947, and commercial flights started a year later. The airport was rededicated as the **JOHN F. KENNEDY INTERNATIONAL AIRPORT** on December 24, 1963, in memory of the 35th president of the United States. Many presidents and dignitaries have visited the airport through the years. In 2016, JFK surpassed **50 MILLION** annual passengers for the first time in its history, and in 2017, that number rose to 54.9 million.

JFK Airport covers 4,930 acres and has six terminals for about 80 different airlines to operate. JFK's four runways total more than **9 MILES**! Visitors to the airport can enjoy numerous restaurants, shops, and services.

CAN YOU FIND...

THE BRONX ZOO

THE BRONX ZOO opened in 1899 after New York City allotted **250 ACRES** of Bronx Park to the New York Zoological Society. **THE BRONX ZOO** is one of the largest wildlife conservation parks in the U.S. and has supported numerous conservation efforts, including a successful campaign in 1907 to save the **AMERICAN BISON** from extinction. The zoo was one of the first to pull animals out of cages, especially with its **LION ISLAND** exhibit that opened in 1940. An aerial tram opened in 1973, a Wild Asia exhibit in 1977, Congo Gorilla Forest in 1999, and Tiger Mountain in 2003.

Today, the zoo houses **4,000 ANIMALS** representing more than **650 SPECIES**. Visitors can still see American bison, lions, gorillas, and tigers, as well as baboons, bears, giraffes, snow leopards, sea lions, various birds and reptiles, and more.

CAN YOU FIND...

WHILE YOU'RE HERE, CAN YOU ALSO FIND THESE OBJECTS?

x5